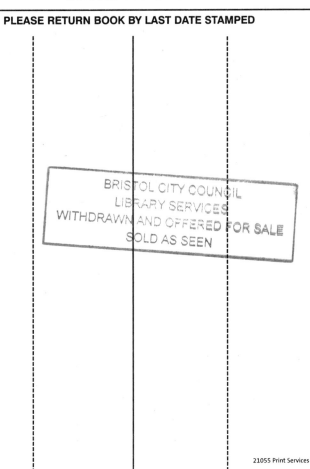

For
Viv

First published 1992 by Walker Books Ltd
87 Vauxhall Walk, London SE11 5HJ

This edition published 2007

4 6 8 10 9 7 5 3

© 1992 Nick Sharratt

The moral right of the author has been asserted.

This book has been typeset in AT Arta.

Printed in China

British Library Cataloguing in Publication Data:
a catalogue record for this book is
available from the British Library.

ISBN 978-1-4063-0987-4

www.walkerbooks.co.uk

The Green Queen

Nick Sharratt

WALKER BOOKS

AND SUBSIDIARIES

LONDON · BOSTON · SYDNEY · AUCKLAND

The
green queen

lay in her
red bed

and looked
at the grey day.

But she had
to go out,
so she got up.

She put
on her blue
shoes,

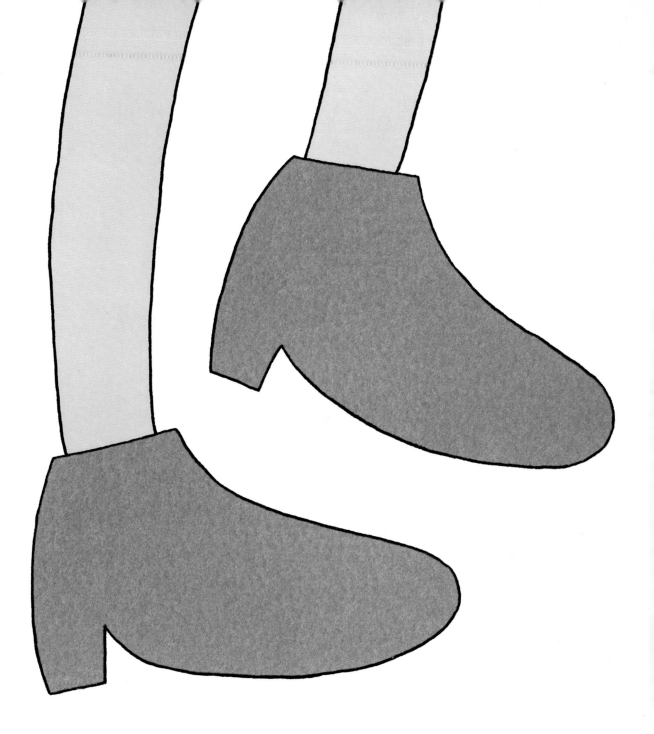

her

black mac,

and her
yellow
and pink
and turquoise
and brown
and orange
and indigo
scarf.
And ...

out she went.